D0191930

GORMY RUCKLES
Monster Contest

GUY BASS
Illustrations by Ross Collins

■SCHOLASTIC

C153746406

KENT
LIBRARIES & ARCHIVES
C153746406

... monster adventures:

Meet the Ruckles

(from a safe distance)

Gormy Ruckles, the monster boy, was very
small, very blue and very hairy. He had
a long tail and just one quite good fang.
Gormy lived at No. 1 Peatree Hill with his
mother, Mogra the Horrid, and his father,
Grumbor the Grim. They were very nice
monsters, as monsters go. But if you do
happen to meet them. . .

. . .try not to get eaten!

To Jennifer Luithlen,
who found Gormy a home!

First published in the UK in 2009 by Scholastic Children's Books
An imprint of Scholastic Ltd
Euston House, 24 Eversholt Street
London, NW1 1DB, UK
Registered office: Westfield Road, Southam, Warwickshire, CV47 0RA
SCHOLASTIC and associated logos are trademarks and
or registered trademarks of Scholastic Inc.

Text copyright © Guy Bass, 2009
Illustrations copyright © Ross Collins, 2009

The right of Guy Bass and Ross Collins to be identified as the author
and illustrator of this work has been asserted by them.

Cover illustration © Ross Collins, 2009

ISBN 978 1 407 10851 3

A CIP catalogue record for this book is available
from the British Library

All rights reserved
This book is sold subject to the condition that it shall not,
by way of trade or otherwise, be lent, hired out or otherwise circulated in
any form of binding or cover other than that in which it is published. No
part of this publication may be reproduced, stored in a retrieval system,
or transmitted in any form or by any means (electronic, mechanical,
photocopying, recording or otherwise) without
the prior written permission of
Scholastic Limited.

Printed in the UK by CPI Bookmarque, Croydon
Papers used by Scholastic Children's Books are made from
wood grown in sustainable forests.

1 3 5 7 9 10 8 6 4 2

This is a work of fiction. Names, characters, places, incidents
and dialogues are products of the author's imagination or are used
fictitiously. Any resemblance to actual people, living or dead,
events or locales is entirely coincidental.

www.scholastic.co.uk/zon

OnE

A Monstrous MooD

It was a hot, sticky day in Janvember, and Gormy Ruckles was in a particularly monstrous mood. The trouble was, he just couldn't find anything really monstrous to do (and there's almost nothing worse than pent-up monstrousness). There was only one thing for it.

Gormy needed a jolly good *roar*.

He wandered around the house, looking for someone to roar at. He found his mother, Mogra, in the pantry, collecting a couple of cows for a monstrous lunch.

Gormy's mother was hairier than any animal she'd ever eaten, and had so many teeth that it took two hours to brush them all. Gormy crept up behind her as quietly as he could. She didn't suspect a thing! He was going to scare her head off! Or at least loosen it. Gormy took two deep breaths into two of his four lungs and

Rooooaaaaar!

"Oh, hello, my little puffball, I didn't see you there. Did you want something?" said his mother, not in the least bit terrified.

"I was. . . No," sighed Gormy, sloping out of the pantry. How could his mother not have been scared out of her fur? Gormy decided that he had roared at everyone on Peatree Hill so many times that his roar must have lost its scariness. He would need to find some other way of being monstrous.

Maybe I'll stomp on something, thought Gormy. *Nothing says "I'm monstrous" like a really stompish stomp!*

Unfortunately, almost everything in the house was much too high for Gormy to reach, and far too big to crush beneath his tiny, blue feet. He made his way into the kitchen and took a monstrously large (and charmingly decorated) plate from the cupboard. He placed it on the floor and lifted his foot into the air. . .

"I hope you're not thinking of stomping on that," said his mother, coming into the kitchen with a cow under each arm. "That plate was a present from your auntie Rogma. She painted the terrified hoomum villagers on it herself. You should know better, Gormy Ruckles."

"But I can't find anything monstrous to do! I hate being stuck on this stupid hill," moaned Gormy.

"Nonsense! There is *plenty* of monstrousness for you to get up to – you just need to use your imagination," said Mogra. "Have you tried in the garden? I could use some help with the weeding. . ."

"Weeding isn't monstrous!" protested Gormy. Actually, monster weeding *was* fairly monstrous, as monster weeds tended to put up a fight (it often took hours of stomping to beat them back into the ground) but that still wasn't enough for Gormy. He tramped grumpily into the garden, looking for something properly monstrous to do. Maybe a really good *throw* would make him feel better. He spotted a plant pot, which looked ripe for a lobbing. He immediately grabbed it in both paws and lifted it into the air with a

"GNnMMMpH!"

"Oi! What's the big idea? I'm sleeping here!" said a small, gruff voice. Gormy looked up at the plant pot to find his best friend, Mike the scuttybug, clinging on for dear life.

As best friends go, Mike was surprisingly disgusting and smelly (even for a creature that only eats poo), but he was the only friend Gormy had ever had.

"Sorry Mike, I didn't see you there," sighed Gormy, placing the pot back on the ground.

"You all right, Gormy?" Mike asked, noticing how droopy-eared his friend was.

"I'm never going to be a real monster!" grumbled Gormy. "I should be out monstering in the land beyond the hill, not stuck here throwing flower pots."

"Cheer up, Gormy, you never know what's around the corner," said Mike, cheerfully. "I mean, one minute you could be going about your day as normal, and the next you might stumble upon a fresh pile of delicious poo!"

Gormy stared at Mike, a little confused. As much as he liked his best friend, Mike did seem to talk about everything in terms of poo.

"My dad'll find me something monstrous to do – *everything* he does is monstrous!" said Gormy, and began walking up the garden.

"Good idea," said Mike, following behind. "He'll know where to find some poo. . ."

Two

Good News

Gormy spotted his father, Grumbor, by the garden shed, lounging on a chair and reading his favourite newspaper, the *Monster Gazette*. Gormy didn't even try to scare his father – Grumbor was much too monstrous to be scared by anything less than the sky falling on his head.

He was at least forty times bigger than Gormy and eighteen-and-a-half times as hairy, and he had more monstrousness in one tail-spike than Gormy had in his whole body.

"How's the monstering coming along?" said Grumbor in a voice so thunderous that it made Gormy's ears tremble.

"What monstering? Nobody's scared of my roar, I'm not allowed to stomp, and I can't find anything to throw! I might as well give up on monstering altogether. . ." growled Gormy.

"Well in that case you certainly won't be interested in *this*," snorted Grumbor, holding up a page from the newspaper.

"*Cow Shortage Leads to Sharp Rise in Goat-Smashing*," Gormy read aloud.

"No, not that – the advert *underneath* it," said Grumbor. Gormy looked lower down the page.

JUNIOR MONSTER CONTEST

Do YOU HAVE WHAT IT TAKES To BE THE MOST MONSTROUS MONSTER BOY IN THE LAND?

A DAY OF

★ MONSTROUS GAMES ★

WILL BE HELD TO DECIDE!

COME TO THE HALF-DEAD TREE IN GOBLOUSE WOOD ON 13th OF JANVEMBER

...AND LET THE CONTEST BEGIN!

Gormy could barely even stay on his two furry feet for all the excitement! A junior monster contest! He'd never even heard of such a thing!

"Still, if you're giving up on monstering, you won't want to bother with some silly monster contest. . ." said Grumbor, folding his newspaper.

"What? No! No, I didn't mean it!" squealed Gormy. "Can we go, please? I'll be the most monstrous monster boy ever, and I'll roar and stomp and throw and smash and crash and be *extra*-monstrous! Can we go, *pleeease*?"

"Oh, stop teasing the boy," said Mogra as she tramped across the lawn. "Of course you can go – we've known about it for ages. That newspaper is three weeks old! The fact is, we think you're ready for a *real* challenge."

"Lesson Six Hundred and Eleventy-twelve: There's nothing like a bit of monstrous competition," said Grumbor. "Now run along and pack your backpack – we leave for the contest tonight."

And with that, Gormy's mother and father linked arms and stamped happily back to the house.

"See, what did I tell you? You never know what's around the corner!" said Mike, as they followed Gormy's parents indoors. "Mind if I tag along?"

"I'm going to a monster contest. . ." whispered Gormy to himself, not quite believing it was happening.

"Great! I'll roll some dung-snacks for the journey." chirped Mike.

Three

The Journey to Goblouse Wood

Gormy realized that he had no idea what
you should pack for a junior monster
contest, so he stuffed his backpack with
whatever he found lying
around. In the
end, he had
packed:

🐾 ONE MOUSE'S TAIL
🐾 FOUR BALLS OF FLUFF
🐾 TWO AMUSINGLY-SHAPED STICKS
🐾 ONE HOOMUM SHOE
(which Gormy's father had got caught
between his toeclaws during a
village-stomping session)

He also packed his **How to be a Better Monster** book, which was full of useful monstering tips from all six hundred and eleven-eleven of Gormy's monstering lessons.

"I hope you've left a scuttybug-sized space in that backpack," said Mike, rolling a dung-ball into the room.

"Climb on in!" squealed Gormy. "Just think, this time tomorrow I'm going to be the most monstrous monster boy ever! And

I'll actually get to meet other monster boys! I might even make new friends!"

"I suppose," said Mike, scuttying into the backpack. "I mean, if you think you *need* more friends. . ."

"Gormy, it's time to go!" called Grumbor. Gormy grabbed his backpack and scampered downstairs. His father was already at the open front door, kissing Gormy's mother goodbye.

"You enjoy yourself out there, Gormy Ruckles," said Mogra, wiping a proud tear from her eye. "And remember, it doesn't matter if you win or lose – it's how you monster that counts."

"Bye Mum!" said Gormy, and raced after his father. The sun was setting as they clambered through the ring of trees that surrounded the house, and emerged in the land beyond the hill.

"There's no time to dawdle – it's a long walk to Goblouse Wood," said Grumbor, and scooped Gormy up in one of his huge, dark blue claws. He dropped him on the top of his head and said, "Hang on tight."

Grumbor set off down the hill at a monstrous pace! Gormy had never really had a Grumbor's eye view of the land beyond the hill before. It made everything look even more impressive than he remembered. This time, however, they travelled *much* further. Mountains that had once seemed far

away now loomed right over Gormy's
head, and torch-lit hoomum villages
were suddenly so close that he could
smell them.

By the time Gormy remembered
to look back, Peatree Hill was nowhere
to be seen. He trembled with nervous
excitement, his head full of monstrous
possibilities.

As dusk turned into night, Gormy
yawned a surprisingly exhausted yawn. He

wrapped his tail around one of his father's horns and nestled into his thick head fur. He drifted off, and his monstrous thoughts turned into monstrous dreams.

Four

So Many Monsters

"Wake up, Gormy – we're here," said Grumbor, stirring him from an excellent smashing dream. Gormy rubbed his eyes in the bright morning sun. He'd slept the whole night! He stretched his tail and looked around. They were in a large, circular clearing of a thick forest.

In the middle of the clearing stood a tall, menacing-looking tree. It was white with no leaves at all, and had been split down the middle by a bolt of lightning. Its gnarled, coiled branches reached towards Gormy like a hundred scary arms.

"So this is Goblouse Wood, eh?" said Mike, poking his head out of Gormy's backpack. "I've never been a big fan of goblice."

"What are goblice?" asked Gormy.

"Only the meanest, most monstrous insect you're ever likely to meet. They give the rest of us a bad name! Look, there's one," said Mike, pointing a tiny leg. On the edge of the clearing, Gormy could see a big, bright yellow ball.

"That's a goblouse? It doesn't look very mean to me," said Gormy.

"They're fine when all curled up and fast asleep, but if you manage to wake one up, then you're in trouble. First they cover you in snot-gobs to make you easier to chew, then *chomp* – you're lunch! Your only chance is to bop them on the nose – it makes them roll back into a ball!"

"I'd bop their brains out!" said Gormy, climbing down from the top of Grumbor's head. But no sooner had his foot touched the dusty floor of the clearing, than the ground started to shake and shudder! It felt like an earthquake!

BOOM! BOOM! **BOOM!**

"**AAH!** What is it?" squealed Gormy, scampering under one of his father's toeclaws.

"Don't panic, Gormy. I think we have company," said Grumbor. As the sound got closer, Gormy realized it wasn't an earthquake at all – it was the sound of monstrous footsteps! Suddenly, twenty-two terrifying monsters emerged from the wood! Each one was as different and frightful as the other. There were hairy monsters, slimy monsters, scaly monsters, and more! Some had arms and legs like Gormy, but others had tentacles, talons, and even flippers!

"So . . . many . . . monsters," said
Gormy, as amazed as he was nervous. The
twenty-two monsters climbed, crawled
and slithered their way into the clearing.
Before long, Gormy was surrounded by
more monsters than he had ever seen. He
watched his father shake claws with one of
them as if they were old friends.

"Grumbor Ruckles, how on Butternut
Hill are you?" the monster asked. It was

huge, hairy and orange, and had three arms and three legs, but just one eye.

"Hello Brog! Mustn't grumble," grumbled Grumbor.

"Blimey, it's a right monstrous get-together," said Mike. "Shame there are no other monster boys here. But then who needs monster boys when you've got old Mike the scuttybug?"

"I . . . I suppose," said Gormy, trying to hide his disappointment.

"And you must be Gormy," said the one-eyed monster, who was called Brog Ump. "I bet you're impatient to meet your competition."

Gormy watched in amazement as twenty-two monster boys appeared from behind the twenty-two monsters' feet! Each one looked like a miniature version of their father or mother, especially the three-armed, three-legged, one-eyed monster boy that appeared from behind Brog Ump's toeclaw.

"I'm Ruggle Ump!" he said. Ruggle was by far the biggest monster boy in the group, and he towered over Gormy. "And I know who you are – Gormy Ruckles! I've heard *lots* about you."

"You – you have?" asked Gormy.

"Of course! In fact, I heard that you're the most monstrous monster boy in the land," said Ruggle.

The thought of anyone thinking he was monstrous filled Gormy with delight, but how could Ruggle have heard of him? He was about to ask that very question when

GROOUAOAAOO AAOAGHH!!!

"AAH!" shrieked Gormy. A roar like that could only come from the most terrifying monster ever!

"OH GOOD, THAT'S GOT YOUR ATTENTION!" boomed an impossibly loud voice. Gormy looked up at the half-dead tree. There, perched in a high branch, was the *least* monstrous creature Gormy had ever seen! He was shorter than the shortest

monster boy, and looked like a piece of
wizened old fruit with fuzzy grey hair
and a hat that was
so long it dragged
behind him.

For some reason, the other monsters (even
Grumbor) stared at him in silent awe.

"WELCOME TO THE ANNUAL JUNIOR MONSTER
CONTEST!" boomed the creature, clambering
down the tree. "I AM YOUR HOST AND JUDGE,
THE OUTSPOKEN OOB!"

"Wow, the Outspoken Oob!" whispered Ruggle in amazement.

"Who's the Outspoken Oob?" asked Gormy.

"You've never heard of the Outspoken Oob, the monster mogul?" said Ruggle. "He's the editor-in-chief of the *Monster Gazette*! It's thanks to him that we have all these junior monster contests. Haven't you been to a monster contest before?"

"Um, yeah, loads!" lied Gormy.

"THERE WILL BE THREE ROUNDS TO THIS CONTEST! AT THE END OF THOSE THREE ROUNDS, I WILL DECIDE WHO IS THE MOST MONSTEROUS MONSTER BOY IN THE LAND!" bellowed the Outspoken Oob. "BEFORE WE BEGIN, ALL MONSTER BOYS SHOULD HANG UP THEIR BACKPACKS ON THE HALF-DEAD TREE. I LIKE TO KEEP MY CONTESTS NEAT AND TIDY!"

Gormy took off his backpack, and went to hang it in the tree . . . but its branches were too high. Even standing on tip-claws, he couldn't reach the lowest branch!

"Here, let me get that," said Ruggle. He took Gormy's backpack, and hooked it on to the branch.

"Thanks," muttered an embarrassed Gormy.

"No problem! I know we're competing against each other and everything, but there's no reason why we can't help each other out. I mean, what are friends for?" said Ruggle, flinging his backpack effortlessly on to the highest branch in the tree.

Did he say "friends"? thought Gormy, beaming from ear to pointy blue ear. "Hey

Mike, did you hear that? I've never had a friend before! A real, monster friend, that is."

"Yeah, he seems all right, I suppose . . . I mean, considering you just met him," said Mike, but Gormy wasn't listening.

"You'd better stay here in my backpack," he said. "There are a lot of monsters around and you don't want to get trampled. I'll come and get you when the contest's over."

"But I thought I was going to help. . ." began Mike, but Gormy and Ruggle had already raced off to the other monster boys, leaving him all on his own. Mike sighed a scuttybug-sized sigh and watched the monster boys gather for the start of the contest.

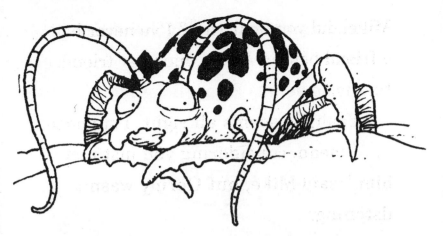

"THE STAGE IS SET!" hollered the
Outspoken Oob as the monsters gathered
around the tree. "AND SO, WITHOUT FURTHER
ADO, LET THE CONTEST BEGIN!"

"Not so fast!" shrieked a horribly
familiar voice. "I want to enter the contest
too!"

Gormy knew immediately who it was.
His excitement turned to horror more
quickly than his mother could turn a
cow into cow pie. Emerging from the
crowd was his arch-enemy, the most

horrible monster boy in the entire
world.

His name was Poggy Boggles.

Five

The Return of Poggy Boggles

Gormy's mouth dropped open at the sight
of Poggy Boggles and his monstrously fat
mother, Volga.

Poggy was Gormy's next-valley
neighbour, and until today, the only
other monster boy he'd ever met. Poggy
was green, hairy, and so horrible that he

made goats seem friendly. All Poggy ever talked about was how incredibly big and monstrous he was, except when he was telling everyone how incredibly small and unmonstrous Gormy was.

"Look, Mummy, there's Gormy Ruckles," said Poggy with a sneer, and threw his backpack easily on to a branch halfway up the half-dead tree. "He's still as tiny as ever, I see! Aren't you *ever* going to grow, Gormy? I've grown a whole inch-and-an-eighth since breakfast!"

"Size isn't everything, Poggy," said Ruggle, looming menacingly over him. Poggy nearly jumped out of his fur! He quickly shuffled behind his mother's fat ankle without another word.

"Ruggle, that was great! I don't think I've ever seen him actually shut up before!"

said Gormy.

"Oh, don't worry about Poggy," said Ruggle. "I met him at the last junior monster contest, and he was just as much of a pain in the tail then. But he's all talk – he's not monstrous enough to beat us."

"Monster boys, line up for round one," boomed the Outspoken Oob. "Parents and guardians, kindly take a seat by the trees and try not to sit on any goblice."

"I've been practising for this contest every day for the last three weeks! How long have you been practising, Gormy?" asked Poggy.

"I. . . Um, well—" began Gormy, suddenly wishing that his parents hadn't kept the contest a surprise.

"When you're as monstrous as Gormy, you don't need to practise," said Ruggle.

"What counts is how monstrous you are in the contest, right Gormy?"

"Right!" said Gormy, so confidently that he almost believed it himself.

Six

Round One: Roaring

With the monster boys all gathered together in the clearing, the Outspoken Oob announced the first round of the contest – roaring!

"How's *your* roar, Gormy? Pretty monstrous, I'll bet," said Ruggle.

"Ha! Gormy couldn't roar his way out of

a paper bag!" scoffed Poggy.

"Speaking of paper bags, here – take one of these," said Ruggle, holding out a small paper bag full of sweets.

"They're called boom-sweets. They make your roar extra loud and monstrous."

Gormy eagerly took one of the boom-sweets and popped it in his mouth. It tasted like rotten eggs and sweaty feet – delicious! As he chewed away, he noticed the Outspoken Oob disappear around the half-dead tree, emerging on the other side with *another* Oob! She was as slow as a Low-Legged Shuffle-Off, and so old and dry that she looked like she might turn to dust at any moment.

"I CALL THIS ROUND THE 'ROAR-SHOCK TEST'!" cried the Outspoken Oob. "THIS IS MY GRANDMOTHER, THE ANCIENT OOB! SHE IS A THOUSAND YEARS OLD, AND STONE DEAF! SHE CAN'T HEAR ANYTHING SHORT OF A THUNDERCLAP! THE MONSTER BOY WHO ROARS LOUDLY ENOUGH FOR MY GRANDMOTHER TO HEAR IS THE WINNER!"

As Gormy waited for his turn, he watched to see if the Ancient Oob would hear any of the roars. And what impressive roars they were!

ROARGH!

after GRaAGH-H!

after RoooORRg!

and even one

BRoOoOoOoOOOG!

Each one was as remarkably monstrous as the last. But the Ancient Oob just sat there, saying things like "SORRY DEAR, DIDN'T CATCH A WORD OF THAT!" and "YOU'LL HAVE TO SPEAK UP!"

"Your turn, Gormy. Show them how it's done!" said Ruggle. Gormy thought that maybe, just maybe he could out-monster Poggy. Maybe he could out-monster everyone! He planted himself in front of the Ancient Oob, took the deepest breath he'd ever taken and. . . **"Squeak!"**

It wasn't a roar at all! Gormy barely even made a noise! The Ancient Oob shrugged in disappointment. Gormy looked around in horror as the other monster boys began to laugh. Where had his roar gone? This had never happened to him before. He took another breath (this time using his spare lung as well) and. . . **"Squeeeak!"**

It was even tinier than before! Gormy slapped his paw over his mouth as the other monster boys fell about laughing!

"Gormy, what's wrong? Are you OK?" asked Ruggle.

Gormy tried to answer, but all that came out of his mouth was, **"Squeak! Squeak! Squeak!"**

"GORMY RUCKLES IS DISQUALIFIED FROM THE ROARING CONTEST FOR FAILING TO ROAR!" bellowed the Outspoken Oob. Out of the corner of his eye, Gormy saw his father sigh and shake his head.

"Disqualified? Dear oh dear, I've never seen anything less monstrous in all my days," chuckled Mrs Boggles.

"Not to worry, Grumbor, some monster boys need more training than others," said Brog Ump. "I could always get my Ruggle to give Gormy a monstering lesson or two."

With the sound of defeat ringing in his pointy blue ears, Gormy sloped off. He couldn't believe it! His first monster contest ever, and he'd messed it up! He looked back to see Poggy Boggles staring right at him and grinning a particularly monstrous grin.

Seven

Round Two: Stomping

Gormy sat under the half-dead tree, trying to work out what on Peatree Hill had happened to his roar.

"What was that all about, Gormy? I've never heard you roar so . . . *squeakily* before," said a concerned Mike from Gormy's backpack.

"I don't know, it just wasn't there! And I was so sure I could do it. . ." muttered a dejected Gormy. "Ruggle must think I'm the least monstrous monster *ever*."

"You're a great monster! You just need to believe it, that's all. Anyway, who cares what Ruggle thinks?" said Mike.

"I care! This was my one chance to make a real monster friend," sighed Gormy. "He even gave me a boom-sweet . . . I'd be surprised if he'll even talk to me now."

"Boom-sweets, eh? Never heard of them. I wonder if—" began Mike, but Ruggle came bounding towards them, wearing the **Most Monstrous Roar** medal. As it turned out, Ruggle's roar had been twice as loud as anyone else's, and the only one that the Ancient Oob could hear.

As bad as Gormy felt, he was pleased that the best monster had won.

"Come on, Gormy, the next round is starting – the stomping contest! If what I hear is true, you'll win easily!" said Ruggle.

Gormy was an excellent stomper. He could smash through a stomp-stone in twelve seconds flat, and once accidentally sleep-stomped his bed clean in half. If he was going to prove his monstrousness, he was going to do it by stomping.

Gormy joined Ruggle and the other monster boys. The Outspoken Oob was waiting with a large bag. He reached in, and pulled out a small, multi-coloured sock.

"WELCOME TO ROUND TWO – 'THE STOMP ROMP'! I HAVE IN MY HAND A 'STOMP-SOCK'. IT WAS KNITTED FROM THE TOUGHEST MATERIALS KNOWN TO MONSTER-KIND! THERE IS ONE SOCK

FOR EACH OF YOU, LABELLED WITH YOUR NAME. THE OBJECT OF THIS ROUND WILL BE TO KEEP STOMPING UNTIL YOU HAVE STOMPED *THROUGH* YOUR STOMP-SOCK! THE MONSTER BOY WHO STOMPS THROUGH HIS SOCK THE FASTEST IS THE WINNER!"

Gormy couldn't remember ever having anything with his name on before, never mind his own stomp-sock! He waited eagerly for his turn to rummage in the sock bag, but when he finally got there, his sock was nowhere to be found.

"I think *this* one's yours, Gormy," said Poggy, dangling Gormy's stomp-sock under his nose. "I found it when I was looking for mine. I didn't even need to read the label – your sock was the smallest one in the bag!"

"Thanks," grumbled Gormy, taking the sock. It was striped in green and purple and had the words **G**ORM**Y** **R**UCKLE**S** written on it.

"Anyway, I hope you have more luck with your stomp than your roar – I've never heard such a pitiful squeak!" added Poggy with a sneer.

"And who's going to beat him? I don't see *you* wearing a medal, Poggy," chuckled Ruggle.

"Oh yeah? Well maybe I – I – oh, forget it!" huffed Poggy. Gormy had never seen him lost for words before! It was better than brilliant!

"MONSTER BOYS, DON YOUR STOMP-SOCKS!"
cried the Outspoken Oob. Gormy squeezed
his furry blue foot into his stomp-sock.
He was immediately surprised at how
uncomfortable it was. At first it started
to itch, and then it started to get hot. In
fact, it got hotter and itchier (and itchier
and hotter!) until Gormy thought his foot
was on fire! He tried to wiggle his toeclaws
around, but that just made it worse!

"PREPARE TO STOMP!" yelled the
Outspoken Oob. "ON YOUR MARKS, GET
SET—"

"YoOOOOOOoWW!!!" screamed Gormy.
His foot was red-hot! He hopped around
the clearing like a horribly hysterical hop-
gobbin!

"Hah! Call that stomping?" sniggered
Poggy.

"Gormy, stop! What's the matter?" said Ruggle as Gormy barrelled into him.

"Hot! hot! HOT!" cried Gormy, bouncing around like a spring-footed Gallumpher! He couldn't help it, his foot felt hotter than a dragon's breath as he rebounded off the other monster boys, knocking them down or sending them flying!

"That boy doesn't know the first thing about stomping! He obviously needs more lessons!" guffawed Mrs Boggles.

"I'm *sure* Ruggle would be happy to give Gormy a monstering lesson or two, Grumbor," added Brog Ump.

"No thank you!" roared Grumbor, and started chasing Gormy around the clearing, doing his best not to trample any monster boys on his way. Finally, as Gormy hopped high into the air screaming "Hot! Hot!" Grumbor caught him by the tail. As he hung in mid-air, Gormy managed to pull off his stomp-sock.

"My foot! It's on fire!" yelled Gormy.

"What do you mean? It doesn't *look* like it's on fire," said Grumbor. Gormy looked down at his foot. Sure enough, it looked just like a foot should – blue and hairy with three claws at the end! What's more, it now felt completely normal, and not in the least bit hot.

"I don't understand. . ." murmured Gormy.

"GORMY RUCKLES IS DISQUALIFIED FROM THE STOMPING CONTEST, FOR FAILING TO STOMP . . . AND FOR UNMONSTROUS SILLINESS!" bellowed the Outspoken Oob. Gormy was so ashamed that he couldn't bring himself to look at the other monster boys, but he could hear their laughter rumble through the trees.

"Honestly Gormy, I don't know what's got into you. You know that's not how you stomp!" barked Grumbor. "We'll talk about this when the contest is over. There's only one round left and I *insist* you don't make any more trouble."

Gormy was about to protest, but he saw

that look in his father's eye which told him
that he was better off biting his lip. As he
shuffled back to the half-dead tree, Gormy
wondered if he had been
wrong all along. Maybe he
just wasn't meant to be
a monster. . .

Eight

Round Three: Throwing

Gormy sat under the half-dead tree and stared at his stomp-sock. How could it have made his foot feel so hot? Then again, it was a *monstrous* sock. Gormy wondered if perhaps he just wasn't monstrous enough to wear it. In fact, he wondered if he was monstrous enough to be a monster at all.

"Let me take a look at that stomp-sock," said Mike from Gormy's backpack. "I reckon there's something funny going on with this monster contest. First your roar, now this! It's as though someone wants to ruin your chances, and I think I might know who. . ."

"What do you know? You're not even a monster," said Gormy grumpily and threw the stomp-sock into the woods. "I got disqualified! Again! I'm useless!"

"Ha! You said it!" laughed Poggy as he strode over. "Poor Gormy, why don't you scurry home and leave the *real* monsters to it?"

"Oh, put a stomp-sock in it, Poggy. Where's *your* stomping medal?" said Ruggle, emerging from behind the tree wearing the **Most Monstrous Stomp** medal. As an embarrassed Poggy scurried off,

Ruggle noticed how forlorn Gormy looked. "Cheer up, Gormy, round three is about to start, and if you're half as good at throwing as I heard, you should win this round easily!" said Ruggle.

There was no doubt Gormy could throw. He could hit a goat with a log at thirty paces, and once threw a pebble so high that it came down with snow on it. It was Gormy's last chance to prove that he belonged in the contest.

"Yeah. . . You're right! I'll throw that rock into next week!" said Gormy.

"Gormy, wait!" called Mike, but Gormy and Ruggle had already joined the other monster boys gathered around the Outspoken Oob.

"Round three – 'the rock chuck!'" hollered the Outspoken Oob, pointing out a long line of twenty-four identical rocks. "THESE ARE YOUR THROWING ROCKS! EACH ONE IS LABELLED WITH YOUR NAME. YOU WILL TAKE TURNS TO THROW, AND THE MONSTER BOY WHO THROWS THE FURTHEST IS THE WINNER!"

As he watched the other monster boys throw their rocks, Gormy knew this was his last chance to show Ruggle, and everyone else, how monstrous he was. He stood behind his rock. It was grey and round, with **Gormy Ruckles** written on it. All in all, it looked thoroughly throwable. He grabbed it tightly, but it felt rather sticky, and left a rock-coloured stain on his hands.

That's weird, thought Gormy. *I didn't know you could get sticky rocks. Still, who knows what rocks feel like this far away from Peatree Hill?*

Gormy lifted the rock over his head. It wasn't even that heavy – this was going to be easy! He reached back and was about to throw when, all of a sudden, he felt the rock move. He looked up, and saw two long antennae pointing back at him.

"Aaaaah!!" he screamed, and dropped the rock!

It immediately began to uncurl. Within moments, it was clear that his rock wasn't a rock at all.

It was a goblouse!

Nine

When Goblice Attack!

Gormy watched in horror as the goblouse uncurled to its full size. It was almost as big as a cow and several hundred times more monstrous. Gormy didn't even have time to wonder why it looked just like his throwing rock before the voice of the Outspoken Oob boomed out over the clearing.

"GORMY RUCKLES IS DISQUALIFIED FROM THE THROWING CONTEST, ON THE GROUNDS OF NON-ROCK THROWING AND BLATANT GOBLOUSE ABUSE!"

"Fancy bringing a goblouse to a throwing contest! That monster boy should be banned from the contest! In fact, ban him from monstering altogether!" screeched Mrs Boggles.

"I *really* think you should let Ruggle give him a monstering lesson," said Brog Ump, but Grumbor wasn't listening.

"Gormy! It'll eat you alive! Run!" he cried, leaping to his feet.

"Eat me?" squealed Gormy, as the goblouse hissed in rage. The monster boys screamed and ran in every direction! This, in turn, made the grown-up monsters panic, and run into the clearing to rescue

their children. Within moments it was a
sea of giant, stamping monster legs and
running, screaming monster boys. But that
didn't stop the goblouse from charging
towards Gormy. Gormy decided that he
should do exactly as his father said – run!

"Watch out for snot-gobs!"
cried Grumbor, desperately
trying to reach Gormy
through the sea of monsters. Sure enough,
the goblouse started firing sticky balls of

yellow snot at Gormy! **SPUT! SPUT! SPUT! SPUT!**

Gormy raced between the snot-gobs and the stampeding legs of the giant monsters trying to rescue their children. He ducked and dodged frantically, as a few misfired gobs splattered other monster boys, **SPUT! SPUT!** covering them in thick, yellowy goo.

Then, suddenly **SPUT!** A snot-gob hit Gormy on the back of the head! He fell to the floor, dazed and confused.

By the time he knew what had happened, the goblouse had zigzagged between the mess of monsters' legs, and was about to pounce on him! Gormy held his breath and prepared for the worst. . . .

"Hang on, Gormy!" came a cry. It was Poggy! He pushed Gormy out of the way, and the goblouse landed on him instead! The goblouse fired a dozen snot-gobs right in Poggy's face, making him an easy to swallow snack!

"Somebody help my little Poggy-woggy!" shrieked Mrs Boggles as she tried to push her way through the monsters.

"Hey, goblouse! Over here!" cried Gormy, kicking the goblouse in the bottom. The goblouse spun around and let out an ear-piercing hiss!

"Uh-oh," said Gormy, wishing he'd thought through taking on an angry goblouse! He turned and ran for the half-dead tree.

It'll never be able to follow me all the way up there! Gormy thought. He leapt on to the trunk, dug in his claws and started climbing, all the while trying to avoid the goblouse's snot-gobs. After a few moments however, the snot-gobs stopped, and Gormy looked back. The goblouse was climbing the tree! He was right behind him!

"**AAH!**" screamed
Gormy, climbing twice as
fast as he'd ever climbed!
This time, Gormy didn't
look back, he climbed
and climbed until
he was almost at
the top of the
tree.

"Gormy,
this way! Up here!"
said a small, gruff voice.
Gormy looked up. There, in the
very highest branch of the tree, was Mike!
He was poking his head out of Ruggle's

68

backpack, which dangled from a thin branch. With the goblouse hot on his furry heels, Gormy clambered on to the branch.

"Crawl to the end! That fat goblouse is too heavy to follow," said Mike. Gormy pulled himself nervously to the end of the branch, hanging on tightly with his claws and tail.

"What are you doing way up here? And in Ruggle's backpack?" asked Gormy, trying not to look down.

"Just doing a little detective work," said Mike. "After what happened to your roar and your stomp, I got to thinking that a certain someone was trying to make you *lose* the contest . . . but I needed proof, so I climbed up here and – look out!" As Mike yelled, Gormy spun around to see the goblouse scramble on to the branch!

"Go away, this branch is full!" cried Gormy. As the goblouse crawled towards them, the branch began to bend and bow under its weight. Ruggle's backpack slipped to the very end of the branch.

"Hang on, Mike!" said Gormy, reaching out to grab the backpack. His claws brushed against the backpack, but it was too late – it slipped off the branch, and fell!

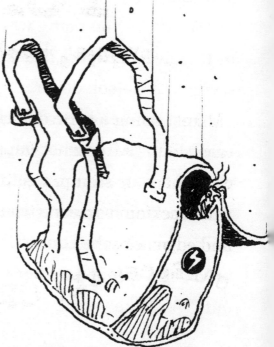

Ten

Ruggle's Backpack

"Mike!" cried Gormy as Ruggle's backpack crashed to the ground! He turned around to climb back up the branch, but the goblouse was blocking his path. It snapped its jaws and edged closer . . .

CREEeeeaAK! CR-A-KAK!

71

"Stop!" cried Gormy, as the branch cracked and splintered. "The branch is going to—"

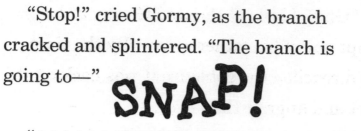

SNAP!

"**AAAAAAAAH!**" Gormy screamed as he fell, expecting to hit the ground. . .

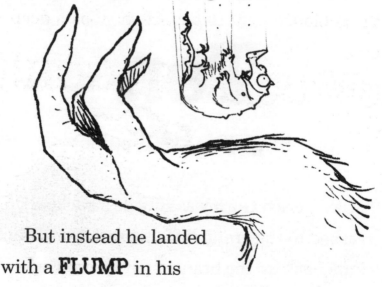

But instead he landed with a **FLUMP** in his father's claw – Grumbor had caught him!

Of course, nobody tried to catch the goblouse, which landed right on top of the backpack!

"Oh no! Mike!" shouted Gormy as he leapt out of his father's claw. By the time he'd reached the goblouse it was back on its feet and angrier than ever.

"Gormy, stop!" cried Grumbor, but Gormy was filled with monstrous rage. As the goblouse went to pounce, he took a deep breath and,

GROOOAAARRGGH!!!

It was the biggest roar he'd ever done, and easily the loudest roar of the contest! The goblouse was almost scared out of its shell, and froze to the spot in terror. Gormy didn't waste any time – remembering what Mike had told him, he lifted his best stomping leg and **BLOMP!** stomped on the goblouse's head, making it curl up into a ball!

"Mike, can you hear me?" he cried, carefully emptying the backpack on to the ground. There, among a host of objects, was his best friend, looking squashed but otherwise intact. Gormy placed him gently in his paw. "Are you OK?"

"Never . . . better. . ." groaned Mike, rubbing his head.

"I thought you'd been squished!" said Gormy, trying not to cry in front of the monsters who had gathered round.

"Oh, it'll take more than a fall from a great height and being sat on by a giant, monstrous insect to knock old Mike out of action," said Mike, then spotted the contents of Ruggle's backpack lying on the ground. "Still, now that I've finally got your attention, look!"

Gormy stared at the strange array of objects. They included:

- ONE BAG OF SQUEAK-SWEETS, FOR THE TEMPORARY REMOVAL OF ROARS
- ONE JAR OF BURNING BLISTER BERRIES, FOR MAKING THINGS FEEL EXTREMELY

HOT, EVEN THOUGH THEY'RE NOT

 TWO TINS OF "ROCK-COLOURED"

PAINT, FOR MAKING THINGS THAT

AREN'T ROCKS LOOK A LOT LIKE ROCKS

(especially goblice)

 ONE FOLDED PIECE OF PAPER WITH THE

WORDS "HOW TO STOP GORMY RUCKLES

WINNING THE MONSTER CONTEST"

WRITTEN ON IT.

"I. . . I don't understand," said Gormy.

"This is what I've been trying to tell you. It was *Ruggle* who made you mess up the contest!" said Mike.

"Ruggle? It can't be. . ." said Gormy.

"Who me? Rubbish! I've never seen any of those things before!"shouted Ruggle,suddenly sweating nervous,  yellow smoke. Gormy picked up the folded piece of paper. "Wait! That's secret! Get your paws off it!" protested Ruggle, but it was too late – Gormy unfolded it.

How to Stop Gormy Ruckles from Winning the Monster Boy Contest
(by Ruggle Ump)

Round 1 - Roaring

Just before Gormy is about to roar offer him a 'Boom Sweet' He'll think it's helping his roar, when it's a roar robbing squeak sweet!

~SQUEAK!

Round 2 - Stomping

Fill Gormy's stomp sock with burning blister berries when he's not looking - his foot will be so HOT he'll never manage a proper stomp!

FIRE

~AAGH!

Round 3 - Throwing

Secretly paint a sleeping Goblouse rock-coloured, put Gormy's name on it and then carefully switch it for Gormy's Rock! Gormy will throw the Goblouse and the Goblouse won't like it one bit!

←Me

"What's going on, son? Did you do all those things?" asked a bewildered Brog Ump.

"Oh, fine, I admit it! I did it all! The squeak-sweet, the burning blister berries, even the goblouse!" cried Ruggle.

"But why? I thought we were friends," said Gormy.

"Friends? Hah! I was only *pretending* to be your friend so I could get close enough to mess things up for you!" yelled Ruggle, madly. "You see, I knew that you were the one monster boy monstrous enough to beat me. . ."

"But how? I've never even met you!" asked Gormy.

"Oh, but I knew all about you!" cried Ruggle. "When I won the *last* junior monster contest, I thought I was the most monstrous monster boy ever, but Poggy Boggles told me he knew someone even more monstrous – the most monstrous monster boy he'd ever met – *you*, Gormy Ruckles! Ever since then, I've been thinking up ways to mess up the contest for you!"

"Ruggle Thasslewinksytweed Ump, you cheated! You can't win by cheating!" cried Brog Ump. "Cheating isn't monstrous, it's . . . it's hoomum!"

"Don't worry, Brog, I'm sure Gormy could give Ruggle a monstering lesson or two," chuckled Grumbor.

Ruggle's father huffed and puffed with embarrassment. He sat Ruggle on a rock, and then made sure all the other monsters could hear him as he explained Ruggle's punishments for cheating. They included:

- NO LEAVING HIS HOUSE ON BUTTERNUT HILL UNTIL HE WAS AT LEAST ONE TENTH-AND-A-SEVENTH
- NO GOATSHAKE, SHEEPSHAKE OR SLUGSHAKE EVER AGAIN
- FIFTY-FOUR LESSONS IN HOW TO BE LESS HOOMUM
- CLEANING THE DIRT AND GRUBS FROM BETWEEN GREAT GRANNY UMP'S TOECLAWS – WITH HIS TEETH!

. . .and thirty-two more. He was nearly at

the end when Ruggle shouted, "You can't make me!" and started scampering across the clearing at top speed.

"Gormy! Ruggle's getting away!" shouted Mike. Gormy didn't waste a second. He grabbed the curled-up goblouse and lifted it over his head.

"Hey Ruggle, catch!" he yelled, and threw the goblouse!

DWONK!

Eleven

And the Winner is . . .

The goblouse soared through the air, curving in a perfect arc and landing right on top of the Ruggle's head. Ruggle fell flat on his face, dazed and defeated. Suddenly the Outspoken Oob appeared through the sea of monstrous legs and strode towards Gormy.

Gormy wondered if he was going to be in more trouble, but as he'd already been disqualified from the whole contest he wasn't too worried.

"Gormy Ruckles, I saw what you just did!" yelled the Outspoken Oob. "And I must say, I have never seen such monstrous roaring, stomping and throwing in all my days! I herby declare you the winner of the junior monster contest!"

"I . . . what? I won?" squealed Gormy.

"You won! Well done, my boy," said Grumbor.

Gormy had never won anything before! (Except that time that Mike bet him he couldn't eat a whole badger in one sitting.) As he swelled with monstrous pride, the Outspoken Oob retrieved the medals from a sore-headed Ruggle. He added the **Most**

Monstrous Throw medal, and then hung
all three around Gormy's neck.

"You did
it, Gormy –
you're the most
monstrous monster
boy in the land!"
said Mike,
proudly. As
the other
monster boys
congratulated
him, Gormy
grinned so hard
that his face
started to hurt. A
moment later, he felt a snot-covered finger
tap him on the shoulder.

"I *suppose* congratulations are in order,"

said a reluctant Poggy Boggles, as he wiped snot-gobs off his face.

"Thanks Poggy . . . and thanks for saving me from the goblouse," said Gormy.

"Well, I owed you that much. If I hadn't told Ruggle how monstrous you were, he would never have tried to mess up the contest for you," said Poggy.

"But why *did* you tell him I was

monstrous? I thought you didn't like me," said Gormy.

"Hah! Just because I think you're monstrous, doesn't mean I *like* you," said Poggy, "and don't think just because I saved you that we're going to be friends either. Next time we see each other, it's business as usual."

"I wouldn't have it any other way," grinned Gormy.

Twelve

Lesson Six Hundred and Eleventy-Twelve
A Little Monstrous Competition

As the sun began to set, Gormy, Mike and
Grumbor set off for home. They made
it back to Peatree Hill by morning, and
Gormy wasted no time telling his mother
all about his victory. She rewarded him
with a mud-covered cow bar and two

glasses of slugshake. Gormy was halfway through the second glass, when he realized how tired he was.

"Monstering can be a tiring business," said Grumbor, as Gormy yawned an exceptionally monstrous yawn. "You've earned a good night's sleep, just like you earned those medals. You're the only monster boy I know who could get disqualified and win a contest in the same day! I was very proud of you today. Now run along, tomorrow is another day for monstering."

With a broad grin, Gormy made his way upstairs and climbed into bed. He was still staring at his medals when Mike scuttied in through the window.

"I've never seen so many medals on one monster," he chirped.

"Glad to see you're feeling better – you look a lot less squashed than before," said Gormy. He thought for a moment and added, "I'm sorry I didn't listen to you about Ruggle. I was so excited about being friends with a monster, I forgot that I've got the only friend I need."

"What? Who? You don't mean *Poggy Boggles*, surely! He's a. . . oh, wait! You mean *me*!" said Mike, blushing a deeper shade of slime-green. "Yeah, we do make a pretty good team don't we? I reckon every monster could use a scuttybug, especially when it comes to keeping an eye on the competition."

"Yeah, and we're going to do even better in the next contest," said Gormy. "I've learned my lessons – remember who your friends are . . . and try not to get eaten by a goblouse!"

Have you read?